This Boxer Books paperback belongs to

. . . .

www.boxerbooks.com

For all the walks with my Papa
S. B.

First published in hardback in Great Britain in 2009 by Boxer Books Limited.
First published in paperback in Great Britain in 2009 by Boxer Books Limited.
www.boxerbooks.com

Text and illustrations copyright © 2009 Sebastien Braun

The rights of Sebastien Braun to be identified as the author and
illustrator of this work have been asserted by him
in accordance with the Copyright, Designs and Patents Act, 1988.

The illustrations were prepared using thin layers of matte acrylic on thick hot press watercolour paper.
The text is set in Adobe Caslon.

ISBN 978-1-906250-80-5

1 3 5 7 9 10 8 6 4 2

Printed in China

All of our papers are sourced from managed forests and renewable resources.

ON OUR WAY HOME

Sebastien Braun

Boxer Books

On our way home,
Daddy raced me.

And I won!

We had to walk through
the dark forest.

With Daddy near me, I wasn't scared.

We tried to count
all the golden leaves
falling from the trees.

High up on
the mountain,

we could see forever.

Down in the valley, we stopped to eat berries.

Daddy said, "It's time to go home," but I didn't want to leave.

The sun was setting.
It really was time to
be on our way.

We ran with the clouds, and our shadows ran with us.

We watched the big yellow sun go down, down, down.

We saw the twinkling
stars come out . . .

And then we were home.

Other Boxer Books paperbacks

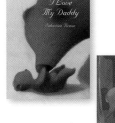

I Love My Daddy & *I Love My Mummy* • Sebastien Braun

Simple, moving words and beautiful illustrations capture the special bond between parent and child in these stunning titles from Sebastien Braun. *I Love My Mummy* and *I Love My Daddy* are celebrations of parenthood for every mother, father and child.

I Love My Daddy
ISBN 978-0-954737-39-3

I Love My Mummy
ISBN 978-0-954737-36-8

Fine As We Are • Algy Craig Hall

Fine As We Are is an exquisitely illustrated story of sibling rivalry. Little Frog is living happily with his mum until the arrival of a multitude of little brothers and sisters. How will he learn to cope?

ISBN 978-1-905417-74-2

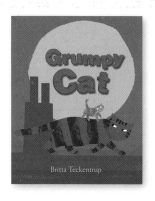

Grumpy Cat • Britta Teckentrup

Cat likes being alone, but a cuddly kitten snuggles up to him and begins to follow him everywhere. At first, Cat tries to shake him off. But when Kitten is in danger, this grumpy cat's true nature is revealed.

ISBN 978-1-905417-70-4

Ha Ba, Baby! • Kate Petty & Georgie Birkett

Ha Ha, Baby! is the story of one very grumpy baby. Just how far will this family go to make their little one laugh? A fun family tale of clowning around.

ISBN 978-1-905417-16-2